Madge Kendal

Dramatic opinions

Madge Kendal

Dramatic opinions

ISBN/EAN: 9783337305178

Printed in Europe, USA, Canada, Australia, Japan

Cover: Foto ©Andreas Hilbeck / pixelio.de

More available books at **www.hansebooks.com**

DRAMATIC OPINIONS.

By MRS. KENDAL.

BOSTON:

LITTLE, BROWN, AND COMPANY

1890.

DAISY, ETHEL, AND DOROTHY.

———•◦•———

AM sure you will be glad to hear I am to have my DRA-MATIC OPINIONS published in America in book form. It is really most gratifying to think the public wish to know my ideas on anything; and I can only hope that in reading them, some other little girls (and boys) will find some bit of experience to amuse them, or advice to guide them, should they ever think of following the theatrical profession.

I am often asked if I wish any of you to go upon the stage; and as you know,

my reply is always the same : Yes, certainly, if you possess sufficient talent ; for
talent you must have, to begin with, sup-
ported by industry, perseverance, good
health, strength of mind, and last, though
not least, a little modesty as to your own
merits.

This is the form of diploma you require
to sign to win the admiration and respect
of the public, — which, when won, and
won worthily, is the greatest honor we can
hope to gain.

Your devoted mother,

MADGE KENDAL.

New York,
  March 14, 1890.

PREFACE.

———❖———

IN offering this little work to the public, during Mrs. Kendal's absence in America, it is necessary to give some explanation of these " Dramatic Opinions," and how they came to be written, — the more so as the form in which the opinions are cast, and the occasional want of regular sequence in the subjects dealt with, have given rise to some criticism and inquiry.

When Mrs. Kendal first undertook to write a series of articles, for " Murray's Magazine," on the profession to which she has devoted her life, and on which she is so eminently qualified to speak, it was agreed that the "Opinions" should be delivered *viva voce*, and should thus, necessarily, partake in some measure of the nature of an "Interview," according to the current acceptance of the term. In this method of treatment it was but natural that some chance allusion made, or question asked, should lead on to a digression, and mar the continuity of the narrative. To eliminate these digressions, however, 'and to rearrange the whole work, would have been to destroy one of its characteristic features.

The interest which the articles aroused, and the favorable criticisms they have met with, have led to their reproduction in this little volume, the readers of which are referred to Mrs. Kendal's own words: "I call these 'Dramatic Opinions,' that if I say anything likely to wound, I may be forgiven. I set down nought in malice, gentle reader; believe them not when they tell you I do."

CONTENTS.

CHAPTER I.

CHAPTER II.

CHAPTER III.

CHAPTER IV.

DRAMATIC OPINIONS.

CHAPTER I.

A Family of Actors. — "Bread and Butter School." — My Father. — My First Part. — My First Earnings. — Mr Ira Aldridge. — My Early Efforts. — Lady Macbeth. — "Matron of the Drama." — Husband and Wife. — French Actors. — French Characteristics. — French Audiences. — Subordinate Parts. — Actors' Difficulties.

MY opinions? What nonsense! they won't interest anyone, for my personal friends already know them, and my enemies won't like them or believe in them;

they will only dissect them, turn them inside out, and try to make out and prove to my unknown generous British public that I am wrong in everything I say! You see, I start with the idea I've enemies. I'll tell you why. All people that have many friends must have the other things; now, I am sure I have the former, so there you are. Who is it says, "A man without an enemy has not got a friend"? Well, I believe that, — that's one of my *opinions !*

Before I begin I suppose I ought to say, like a child on going into school, how old I am, and where I was born. But, dear reader, please don't ask me that, — where I was born, and how old am I. Don't you know? Some folks add a year or two to my age when writing about me, and can't quite decide whére I was born. Perhaps I " growed," eh? I sha'n't tell you, because curiosity in a man is awful; in my sex it's pardonable, I 'm told, and most women ask each other, " How old do you think Miss or Mrs. So-and-so is? Now think. She began in such a theatre, and played such a part; she must have been over twenty then,— that makes her — Oh, my dear, she *must* be ! " But *men* never talk like that. At their clubs they converse only of politics, and discuss the progress of the different ages of man; but'no, never, never of woman !

Both my father and mother were on the stage; so were my grandfather and grandmother; so were my great-grandfather and great-grandmother;

so were my great-aunts and uncles, my *simple* aunts and uncles, my brothers, my sisters, my nephews, my nieces.   I hardly have a relation in the world that has n't been on the stage, except the new-made knight, Sir William Tindal Robertson, the member for Brighton; but his father, my uncle, was an actor for some years.

We are very, very proud of the fact, — when I say "we," I mean the Robertson family.   *We* sounds regal, doesn't it? But I can't say *us*, because that would n't be grammatical ; so I am obliged to say *we*.   Yes, we are proud of it. The blood of the Montmorencys does n't fire up more when they speak of their long line of ancestry, dating from the Conquest, than the Robertson blood burns with enthusiasm when speaking of our long

line of descent from actors of old.
And we shall, I hope, do nothing in
the future to lessen that enthusiasm.

I am the twenty-second child of my
parents. Yes, the twenty-second.
My brother Tom, the author, was my
father's eldest son. I am the youngest
of the family. I never knew my
brother Tom except as a man grown
up, such a great many brothers and
sisters came between us.

I am sorry to say I did not play in
any of his comedies,— in none of what
is considered his best work. I played
in " Dreams " at the Gaiety, which
was charming to the end of Act II.,
and then fell off considerably, — and
none knew this better than himself.
I often hear my brother's work
spoken of as " The Bread and Butter
School." Bread and butter, — but

what good bread and butter! How
fine the flour! How carefully knead-
ed, and always served hot from the
bakehouse! Then the butter! How
fresh and sweet; what an excellent
color, what delicate pretty pats, with
just enough salt to give it a rich,
delicious flavor! .And then, again,
how well the butter was spread over
the bread, — just enough, no more!
And this bread, like all good home-
made loaves, was all the better for
the keeping. Everybody must eat
bread and butter; then how necessary
these commodities should be whole-
some and pure! We Robertsons
never speak of Tom without calling
him Napoleon, for his " Bread and
Butter School" was the *coup d'état*
to many things. Sometimes I fancy
people mean to be rude, and speak

slightingly of his work when they call it " bread and butter; " but at every tea-party I take my children to, I say, " Begin with your uncle's fare *first;* you shall have some fairy, poetical drama called ' cake ' afterwards! "

Now let me say a few words of personal biography.

Once upon a time there were three theatrical circuits, — the York circuit, the Bath circuit, and the Lincolnshire circuit. A Robertson built theatres in the eight towns of the Lincolnshire circuit ; companies used to travel, as we do now on a larger scale, among the provincial towns; but in those days all the theatres within a certain radius belonged to one manager, and you were an actor of importance if you belonged to either circuit. My uncle, who was known as " old Tom

Robertson the Mogul," succeeded to the property; when he died he left it to his wife, from whom my father obtained it.

Mr. Chippendale, Messrs. Compton, Braid, and Rogers, of the Haymarket Theatre, were all actors in my father's theatre. I have letters from Compton to my father when he began —I do not like to say at how much a week, and how he was advanced a certain sum of money to get to town. Afterwards life was reversed; and when I became an actress at the Haymarket Theatre, I was called by these old actors " the daughter of the regiment."

When the railway mania, or some other burst of speculation, reached into Lincolnshire, my father lost everything he possessed; and on the very day and hour when he knew everything was lost, I was born.

As I have told you, I was the youngest of the family, and considered a very wonderful person to have been reared, because I was the twenty-second child of the same parents. My mother's maiden name was Elizabeth Marinus. She was a German, — the name is Dutch. She was born near the Hague, but her parents really were Germans. Mr. Buckstone was at one time, I believe, a sweetheart of my mother's, and he was so thin and so small that my mother used to say she could blow him away! I always have believed (perhaps it is a childish belief) that if my mother had had a fair opportunity of appearing before the London public, she would have been a very

shining light indeed. I believe she
did act there once, but not in any
prominent part. She was a true
comédienne. I was too young to
form a reliable estimate of her powers
until she was quite an old woman;
but her reminiscences and her anec-
dotes and her sense of humor were
very fine.

It appears that my mother wrote
to Mr. Chute, of Bristol, and said:
"You were a poor actor once in our
theatre; you have now one of your
own, — let me be an actress in it."
Mr. Chute said, "Yes;" and in that
theatre I was brought out as Eva, in
"Uncle Tom's Cabin."

Gentlemen who acted with me were
George Melville, William Rignold,
and George Rignold. A clever lady,
Miss Cleveland, who now is Mrs.

Arthur Stirling, was the Eliza. I was cast for the part of Eva, which contained three or four little songs, because I used to sing as a child, and was supposed to have something of a voice. At the end of the play I used to be carried up to heaven with Uncle Tom. I was put in a kind of machine, something was put round my waist, and I went up in a sort of apotheosis, as in " Faust and Marguerite." I remember too that all my hair was let down my back. I was very fair when I was a child. You can imagine that; as one grows older, hair gets darker if nature is not interfered with.

Then came a blank in my life, when I was too old to play children's parts, and not old enough to play women's. There was a certain Miss

Pillinger, an intimate friend of Mrs. Chute's, who used to keep a musical academy of very great pretensions. From Miss Pillinger I received — I must not say my musical education, because I am not a sufficiently good musician to say that, but the elements of one.

I remained at Miss Pillinger's Academy until I was about fifteen, when Mr. Wild, who was a partner of Mr. Buckstone at Bradford, came and heard me sing, and insisted on engaging me for the burlesque boy's part of Rasselas. Mr. John O'Connor was the scenic artist. He used to do painting on his own account. I said to him one day, " Mr. O'Connor, when I am rich I shall buy a picture from you ; " and the first five pounds I ever spent on a picture was in buying a bit of still life of his, which now hangs in my drawing-room.

At this time I used to play parts in the first piece, the burlesque boy's part in the second, and then I sang; and nobody could discover whether I was going to be an actress or a singer, or what my future was to be. I was always told I was " going to be some-thing ; " and perhaps the most tangi-ble result of the prediction was that during this period of my life I began to earn £10 a week. I was very glad and happy, because I then took my father and mother off the stage, and never allowed them to act again.

I had for some time been very anxious to do this. One day an old actor had come off the stage and said, " God bless my soul, Robertson has forgotten his lines again ! " I thought,

"They shall work no more." From that time my father and mother never acted again.

After leaving Bradford, I came to London, and played for six weeks at the Haymarket Theatre with Mr. Walter Montgomery. The Hon. Lewis Wingfield played Roderigo; he was a great friend of my brother's, and a great lover of art in every way. During the time that I was there, Mr. Ira Aldridge was engaged to act. Mr. Ira Aldridge was a man who, being black, always picked out the fairest woman he could to play Desdemona with him, not because she was capable of acting the part, but because she had a fair head. One of the great bits of "business" that he used to do was where in one of the scenes he had to say, "Your hand,

Desdemona." He made a very great point of opening his hand and making you place yours in it; and the audience used to see the contrast. He always made a point of it, and got a round of applause, — how, I do not know. It always struck me that he had got some species of — well, I will not say " genius," because I dislike that word, as used nowadays, but gleams of great intelligence. Although a genuine black, he was quite *preux chevalier* in his manners to women. The fairer you were, the more obsequious he was to you. In the last act he used to take Desdemona out of bed by her hair and drag her round the stage before he smothered her. You had to wear sandals and toed stockings to produce the effect of being undressed.

I remember very distinctly this drag-
ging Desdemona about by the hair
was considered so brutal that it was
loudly hissed. Those are the main
points of my performance in "Othello," to the success of which I am
afraid I did not very much con-
tribute.

Now I must tell you something
very odd. Madame Jenny Lind,
afterwards Madame Goldschmidt,
once called on me and told me she
was going to teach the scholars of
the Royal College of Music, by the
wish of His Royal Highness the
Prince of Wales, and she did not
feel that she would be able to teach
them to sing unless I would teach
them how to speak. I told her I
did n't consider myself qualified to do
so, whereupon she replied that she

would not. belong to the College of
Music unless I did. I was so immensely flattered by this great and
gifted creature coming to me that on
the receipt of what I am proud to
think was a command from H. R. H.
the Prince of Wales, who, you know,
is the President, I undertook to teach
the scholars that came to Madame
Jenny Lind. Well, when I first called
over the names of my pupils, I found
the name of " Miss Aldridge," and was
informed that she was the daughter
of the gentleman with whom I had
acted Desdemona as a girl at the Haymarket, — a fact which immediately
gave me the strongest interest and
feeling for her. She has since then
given singing-lessons and concerts.

From the Haymarket I went with
Mr. Montgomery, and opened the

new Nottingham Theatre, which he had taken. Nottingham was one of the places where my grandfather had built a theatre. It was a strange thing that my eldest sister sang the last note in my grandfather's theatre, and that I sang the first note in the New Theatre Royal. Again, you see, I go back to my singing propensities. I sang the first verse of " God Save the Queen," which in those days was always upon the programme. I was in Nottingham for a very short time. From there I went to the Theatre Royal, Hull, which was a new theatre, to open with Mr. William Brough, who was the manager. I was the leading lady. I used to play everything, from Lady Macbeth to Papillonnetta. Papillonnetta was a lady with wings, in a burlesque of

Mr. Brough's. The wings were invented by Mr. Brough, and they used to wind up and flap for about ten minutes, and you then had to run off and be wound up again. In that I used to dance a *pas seul*. Every actress on the stage of any known position has always attempted Lady Macbeth, and has got a more or less ridiculous or interesting anecdote to tell of that attempt. Here is mine: Mr. Samuel Phelps came down to Hull to play for three nights, Thursday, Friday, and Saturday. He chose for his three nights' performances "Richelieu," in which I played Julie; the "Man of the World," in which I played the comedy part; and to complete it, Lady Macbeth.

The reason I played Lady Macbeth was that there was nobody else to

play it, except a very old lady.
Mr. Phelps had to choose between
this very old lady and myself. Mr.
Brough told Mr. Phelps that he had
better take me, as whether I could
do it or could not, I had at that time
so completely got the Hull people to
like me that they would forgive me
anything. I was put in a garment of
my mother's. Mr. Brough, thinking
that this was a hazardous experiment,
put it in the play-bills " for the first
time." I went on, and was received tre-
mendously; and having been taught
by my father, I suppose I got through
it somehow, and was vociferously
cheered. It shows how if anybody,
however incompetent, pleases an audience, they will sweep art, experi-
ence, and knowledge out of the whole
thing, and give the inexperienced a

hearing. I was called over and over again. Mr. Phelps did not take me before the curtain. Why should he? When he went on again, he was greeted with the most tremendous cries of "Bring her out!" As my father was standing at the wings, he was sent for, and a young man out of the gallery, of enormous size, came round and said to him, "Ay, Mr. Robertson, if thou say'st t' word, I 'll duck him in t' Humber; he 's not brought on our Madge." My father had to take Mr. Phelps out of the front door to avoid the gallery boys throwing him in· "t' Humber." A greater insult to a "genius" — for this time we may apply the word in its right place — a greater insult than a chit attempting to stand upon the same stage with this man, who was, as all the world will acknowledge, a really great actor, I have never experienced. But so kind, so generous was Mr. Phelps that when I came to London he paid me the compliment of sending for me to play Lady Teazle at his benefit at the Standard Theatre.

From Hull I came to the Haymarket Theatre under Mr. Buckstone, where I remained seven years. There I met my husband and married. I went to the Haymarket a single girl, and left it the "Matron of the Drama." This title, which is always applied to me, it would be foolish to say I am not proud of. I am very, very proud of it; but with the pride comes a feeling of regret at being so conspicuously selected. To the generous-minded friends who have given me this title, my grateful thanks are due;

but I fear they did not take into consideration the feelings of many others when they placed on my poor head this crown of honor! I next went to the Court Theatre with Mr. Hare to play Lady Flora; then to the Prince of Wales's to play in " Peril " and " Diplomacy; " and afterwards to the St. James's. Such has been my life. They say that rolling stones gather no moss, but sometimes I think it is a pity to remain too stationary.

I have often been asked, I may say by thousands, both in letters and in conversation, as a matter of interest by my friends and from curiosity by others, why my husband and I always act together, and have never been parted. I wish to state to the public why it is so. My father was an actor who said he believed that the greatest

amount of domesticity and happiness
in a life devoted to art could exist
upon the stage, provided husbands
and wives never parted. If, on the
contrary, a man, because he could
earn £10 a week more, went to one
theatre, whilst his wife for a similar
reason went to another, their interests
tended to become divided, their feelings ran in separate grooves, and grad-
ually a shadow would grow up at
home which divided them forever.
On my expressing a wish that I should
marry an actor, he said that only on
this condition would he allow me to
marry my husband, — that we should
never be parted. Mr. and Mrs. Charles
Kean always acted together, and she
indorsed my father's words. If my
husband and I had been separated; if
he had played parts to other women;

if other women had played parts to
him, and I to other men, and other
men to me, — there is no doubt that
certain go-ahead people would have
preferred it, and we should probably
have been worth thousands of pounds
more to-day.   But, on the other hand,
there is another section of the public
who say they like to see us act
together; that the very fact of knowing we are man and wife, gives them
a certain satisfaction in witnessing our
performance, which they would not
otherwise feel.   That, however, I must
leave for the public to decide; as far
as we are concerned, however, it was
a vow made to my father, from which
my husband has never departed; and
if, when we are dead, we leave our
children less money, let us hope they
will respect what we have done.

Letters have been written to me and friends have come to me and argued the point, saying it would be more interesting to see another man embracing me. Where the interest comes in, I do not know. Also that it would be infinitely more fascinating if somebody else acted with my husband. I believe there is a little sort of story going forth that the reason of all this is to be found in the existence of a peculiar green-eyed monster in Mrs. Kendal's heart. Poor lady! It is a blessed gift that her shoulders are broad, because I have found that if a woman has lived many years happily and creditably with her husband, some reason or reasons must be given. However, in return, I beg the disaffected always to look with large opera-glasses at my husband,

who, having lived with me for twenty
years, is a very good target for them
to shoot their pistols at!

I wonder will it interest you to hear
what I think of the French actors
coming over to London, and the effect
it had on art generally in this country?
I think for one thing that it has made
the English people see that there is
just as much good art here as abroad.
But then you must make allowances
for the different peculiarities of na-
tions.   For instance, as you drive
through the streets of Paris you often
see two people talking at a corner,
and you notice their gesticulations.
One is explaining something to the
other. From the extraordinary twin-
kle in his eye, the expression of his
mouth, the waving of his hand in the
air, and the undulating sort of move-

ment of his body, you suppose that
he is describing some most exciting
scene, perhaps a murder; you go up
to him, and find that he is simply
pointing to a *café* where he had some
beer! Now, all these gesticulations
are to a Frenchman perfectly natural;
he is to the manner born.

We English, speaking generally,
have by nature no gesticulation.
We are more phlegmatic, more solid.
Like the parrot, we " think a great
deal," but we don't show it. We sit
on our perches and imagine we are
expressing all sorts of emotions, but
as a matter of fact we are doing no
such thing. Our excitement is taken
inwardly; inwardly we feel as much
as the French do, perhaps more, —
but we do not give that extraordinarily
graphic description of what is passing

in our minds which makes a Frenchman's account of even trivial events
so dramatic. Therefore I consider
that the gesticulation on the French
stage, which is supposed to be so
wonderful and so charming, is merely
the result of a difference in national
temperament. With us it is more
art than nature; with them it is more
nature than art. As animated gesticulation is more difficult of attain-
ment by English actors, it ought,
when we do see it, to be estimated
doubly highly from an art point of
view. But there is another reason
why we pay less attention to the
small details of gesture. English audiences are so totally different from
French audiences. I remember going
to see a play called " Les Danischeff,"
where one of the greatest actresses,

Madame Favart, played the part of the mother. She was a *grande dame*, and came on the stage with two attendants, — a parrot and a dog. For a long time she held her audience by little remarks such as " My son has arrived in Paris. Pleasant society there. I was there myself in my youth. I enjoyed it immensely; " then to the parrot, " you darling," — and so she went on. She just played with her little bits of lace on her dress, put her rings straight, arranged her bracelets, took her lace pocket-handkerchief up and sprinkled a little scent, fanned herself, played with the dog, conversed with the parrot, spoke of the political intrigue that was going on in Russia. There was not any action, any " play; " but the artist arrested the atten-

tion of the audience, who sat listening eagerly to nothings exquisitely
delivered.

An English audience would have
grown impatient; they would have
said, " There is nothing going on,
there is no conversation, there is no
narrative, there is no action."

French audiences will listen atten-
tively to long duologues, or even
monologues; witness the monologue
in " Don César de Bazan," and that
oration of Charles V. to the tombs of
his fathers in " Hernani." When I
heard it, it was magnificently delivered by M. Worms. It lasted — my
gracious, how long it lasted! Nothing took place, the actor was surrounded by tombs; a dark scene, a
beautiful soliloquy in verse, and the
audience listened to the music of

their own language, delivered by an elocutionist whom to hear was a delight.

Now, an English audience must have action. The eye must be pleased or the ears tickled; there must be some strong appeal to the senses. You must gratify the eye by spectacle, or the ear by an equivoque; some such devices are indispensable. In France you hear two or three men and women discuss some political question or society question of the day for twenty minutes or half an hour, as they do, for instance, in the play of " Le Monde où l'on s'ennuie." Such is the difference between an English and a French public.

I have often been asked whether actors who play minor parts conspic-

uously well, spring suddenly into
more prominent positions. The question reminds me of an incident which
occurred in a play by Arthur Sketch-
ley, the well-known author of the
" Mrs. Brown " series. He had written
a three-act drama called " Blanche,"
which my husband and I, on tour at
the time, were playing at the Alex-
andra Theatre, Liverpool. The plot
was taken from an old French drama,
and consisted of a woman being
falsely accused of poisoning her husband. ·It was very hard work, I remember, for three acts for every one
in the play. In the last scene, when
the villain steps forward and de-
nounces the heroine with the words,
" You poisoned your husband ; I saw
you put the poison in the glass at
such and such a time," a black man-

servant comes forward and says,
"Liar!" I am sorry to say that this
was the only occasion for genuine
applause throughout the play. So
great was the success of the minor
actor that he immediately jumped
into a most prominent position in the
provinces, and became a leading man.
Whether he has kept his position till
now, I do not know, for I have lost
sight of him.

Many actors have established re-
putations by playing small parts
only, and by playing them so well
that, of course, being known for a
particular style of acting, they are
engaged solely for the kind of parts
that suit their peculiar personalities.
In this way they sometimes establish
a good reputation, and are really
more valuable than some persons in

greater positions. As to the income they can earn, it is hard to lay down a general rule. There are men in our profession, and women too, who have played subordinate parts, and who, when fitted physically and artistically for them, are worth their weight in gold. They earn an extremely large sum of money while they have an engagement; but the engagement is so precarious and breakable, according to the arrangement, — whether it be for the play, which may or may not be a success, or for whatever time it may be. In a bank, when a man has once arrived at being the manager, he gets so many hundreds a year, and it goes on until he dies or does something unworthy of the trust of his employers. We actors and actresses

4

are but "creatures of the hour," and if we do not make money while before the public, we certainly make nothing when we are hidden from their admiring eyes.

Perhaps you want to know whether there have been any public favorites who never could really fill a prominent position or take a leading part in a play, but who have made a small part famous? I think I may safely say that there have not, because directly a man has made a success, he immediately gets on and on and on. There is no station at which you take the train "forever" in our profession. You see the man who made his reputation by the one word "Liar" did not go on lying, — he jumped. On the other hand, there is no difficulty in finding actors to take

small parts; the difficulty is to know
whom to refuse nowadays. All these
matters are easily arranged. There
is no difficulty in anything when you
are down in the world; difficulties
only begin when you rise to a position. As long as you are a nobody,
you hurt nobody, and therefore you
are a charming person and all right.
It is when you are in a position,
when others want that position, and
when, if they cannot say one thing
against you, they wish to devise
something else, that difficulty comes
in.

CHAPTER II.

PEOPLE often ask me what
are the secrets of popular-
ity in an actor. Who can
say? It is that little *something* which
we cannot describe which makes him
or her sympathetic with an audience.
If we could say *what* it is, if we could,
as it were, place our hands on the

actual spot and declare it to be this
or that which gives popularity, should
we not all try and get it for ourselves?
Were it to be sold in a shop, should
we not go and buy it? It is that
little mysterious something which
makes a man or woman great or
popular. They may be full of faults,
they may have any strongly marked
individuality you like, it is that
"something." that unknown quality,
which makes them more or less sympathetic. To a certain extent the
public is led by the voice which says,
" Follow me ; this or that is great."
Many actors have arrived at popularity by the public being told they are
great till it comes to believe them so.
At the same time the public are so
marvellously intuitive, they are so
wonderfully correct, that a man could

not sustain his popularity, or a woman sustain hers, — and by " sustain " I mean go on for a period of years retaining their popularity, — unless there were that " something " in them.

How often one goes into a theatre and sees in the programme the name of a clever man or woman playing a second or third rate part! We say, " Oh! Mr. So-and-So, or Mrs. So-and-So. How delightful! they always act so well." But for all that they are not the particular person who has taken us to the theatre, they are not the person whom we have paid our money to see. We are delighted when we see their names on the programme, but they have not attracted us there. The actor or actress who attracted us there may not be half so good an artist, but

he or she possesses the indefinable
" something" that draws, — draws us
not only from a monetary, but also
from a sympathetic, point of view.
There are many good actors and actresses who intellectually could teach
those whom the public have placed
in a position above them, but who
lack that extraordinary power of
drawing. You cannot tell what it
is, this particular charm, it is inde-
scribable. Perhaps, my reader, you
suggest that it is genius in some form
or other. No, that is not the right
word. The word " genius" should
strictly only be applied to about
three of the people I have met in the
whole course of my life. It is true I
have heard it applied at least three
million times, — thrown broadcast, in
fact; so that for me it has rather

lost its meaning. No, it would be impossible to describe the secret of popularity in an actor or an actress.

Some people say that when you are acting upon the stage with an actor or actress you think they are good, and yet their art does not go " over the footlights " and reach the heart of the public. Sometimes I have been told, " How bad this actor is at the rehearsal? and close to you, how unsympathetic; and yet what an effect he produces on his audience!" I do not believe this. I do not believe that any actor who is not sympathetic to act with, — and by this I do not mean anything but actually the word I am using, sympathetic in his part, — I say I do not believe that such an actor's art *can* reach the public. If the tone of an actor's or

actress's voice with whom you are
acting does not allow you to answer
them in the frame of mind and heart
that you should be representing while
you speak, and is not in sympathy
with you, it is impossible for you to
make the audience follow your train
of thought. Acting is like photo-
graphy. One single person has in-
stantaneously to photograph the same
impression upon the minds of hundreds. It is the duty of an actor to
make the audience see the part from
his point of view. If the audience is
discussing whether the actor is right,
the actor has not got hold of them.
When I am acting, I must make the
people feel that they see it from *my*
point of view. If they discuss during
the time I am acting whether I am
right or wrong, I certainly have not

got hold of them. They may discuss it afterwards, and say, " He was
right," or " She was wrong," — this,
that, and the other; but during the
time I am acting, it must be, as it were,
a photograph thrown upon each individual mind of the audience, and I, or
whoever is acting, must have the power
to impress each mind so forcibly that
for the time at least it must see only
the situation as it is so focussed.

This is one of the difficulties in
playing a part taken from a well-
known book. Each person among
the audience, on reading the book,
has drawn his own picture of the
character. When they come to see
an actor or an actress play that
character, they immediately question
whether it is right. " She did not do
that. In the book I see so and so.

He did not do so and so." Of course this difficulty is at its height when one is playing Shakspeare. It does great credit to the talent of the actor or actress if they realize to the *majority* the idea of the characters they have read of.

I am not now considering the truism that the playing of an actor ought not to appear to be playing at all, but a scene in real life. That is naturally a *sine qua non*. I am thinking of the cases where the public have read about a character in a book and formed their own ideas about it. A fine actor's interpretation of such a character ought to appear true to the majority of the audience, and be sympathetic to every intelligent conception of the part. The only person I ever saw who realized my idea of Jo in "Bleak House" was Miss Jenny Lee. She was so physically like the part, and it was such a beautiful performance, that one never questioned it; it was the reality. But it is very, very difficult, when the majority of the public have read a book, for an actor to realize for them what they have already realized for themselves, often in various ways. To take an illustration. I can only call to mind two painters who have succeeded in realizing the ideal we may have formed of the face of our Blessed Lord. How often painters try to give the sublimity, the intellectuality, the divinity of that face! Yet when we stand before their pictures, how seldom do they come up to our imaginative ideal, because we each have our own! There is always something lacking. Something of the same kind may be said to be true of representations of Shakspeare's characters.

And then there is the difficulty of rightly understanding the text. Get any three actors — three Shakspeare students — to go and see a performance of Shakspeare. Each one will discover a new reading, or at any rate converse and argue and cavil about the emphasis. For instance, Othello says: "Put out the light, and then — put out the light." Now, I have heard the most clever and intelligent and gifted men in my profession argue — I had almost said for hours — over the reading of these few words, "Put out the light, and then — put out the light." One maintained that Shakspeare's meaning is,

"Put out the light," — referring to the light of Desdemona's life; "and then," — as if Othello had already in thought killed her, and asked himself afterwards the question, "Put out the light?" Another asserted that "Put out the light" refers to the candle which Othello carries in his hand. "Put out the light," — that is, extinguish the candle; "and then" referring to the murder he is about to commit. Who shall decide which interpretation is correct? Who shall say what was in Shakspeare's mind when he put into Othello's mouth the words, "Put out the light, and then — put out the light"? There are hardly two men or women in my profession who would be found to agree upon the reading of that one line. I can only tell you that I have heard it discussed so often that I scarcely know what my own opinion on the subject is. And Shakspeare is full of such lines. His mind was so subtle, so extraordinary, that I can quite understand this eager discussion going on centuries after his death as to whether he really wrote the plays which bear his name, or whether he did not. The more you know of Shakspeare, the more you read of him, the more marvellous does he appear, and the more subtle. " How noble in reason, how infinite in faculty! In action, how like an angel; in apprehension, how like a god! " Read Shakspeare when you are young, read Shakspeare when you grow older, and the same words will seem to have totally different meanings. The phrase in the Bible,

" Now we see through a glass darkly,"
might be applied to the reading of
Shakspeare's plays. It would be
impossible for any ordinary persons,
if they were to live to be hundreds
of years old, and thought only of cul-
tivating their minds, to tell you, from
their own small range of thought,
what Shakspeare meant. This will
help you to appreciate the tremendous difficulty of realizing the ideal-
ity and personality of Shakspeare's
characters.

However, every writer of plays is
not a Shakspeare, and sometimes —
indeed, I may say often — a poor play
can be turned into a success by fine
acting. There is one matter upon
which I venture to quarrel with some
of the chief critics of our time. They
never point out to the public where

the author ceases, and where the
actor begins, — where the author has
" made " the actor, and where the
actor " makes " the author. The di-
viding line is so fine that even the
best writers of our time fail to discern
it, and it would be impossible for *me*
to attempt to define it here. A writer
brings a play into a theatre, and, as it
were, leaves his child in that unknown
region. It is in the manager's dis-
cretion to cast that play as he thinks
best, and for the stage director to
bring out all the author's points. It
is to a very great extent to the stage
management that the success of the
play is due. Then comes the expo-
sition by the actors. I have seldom
met an author who has not said, " I
do not think you make enough of
this; I meant this to be very much

greater in effect;" and as often — no, perhaps not *quite* so often — he says, "I never thought, when I wrote that, that there was so much in it as you have made of it." One man has said these two things to me. It is not every author, clever men as authors are, who knows exactly what effects will be produced by his play. He has his own ideas, and he sometimes owes a great deal to the actors. A certain author, whom I will not name, is accustomed to declare, "I do not want actors and actresses to think what they are going to do with my parts. These are my lines as I have written them: let my ideas be reproduced; let us have no vagaries of other people's." But that author has never succeeded in touching the heart of his public. When a writer leaves

his play in a theatre, he gives it up,
as it were, and, in my opinion, it
should be left to the feelings of
the artists engaged in it, who as a
rule work most wonderfully together.
They ask each other's opinions, con-
sult each other's thoughts, and in-
advertently teach one another by
suggesting little details, and, as it
were, threshing out the meaning of
the author's words, sometimes wonderfully improving the play in the
process.

I have known adverse criticism to
be useful in many instances. One
strikes my memory very vividly.
When first the play of "Lady Clan-
carty" was produced at the St.
James's Theatre, I think nearly all
the criticisms upon me were adverse;
in some cases the writers — gentle-

men in whose opinion I have the greatest faith, and for whose judgment I have the greatest admiration —pointed out most kindly to me where they thought my reading and my view of the character were wrong. First impressions had been made by a very beautiful and extremely talented woman; and I daresay that to some extent militated against me, — for first impressions always are the strongest, and it is quite right they should be. I felt so instinctively that these criticisms were right that I worked very, very hard at my part for weeks and weeks. I went on a long tour with it in the country, and tried it in many different ways; and eventually, when I returned to reopen the St. James's Theatre in the winter season with it, the criticisms

of me were most generous and kind,
and I was highly praised for the im-
provement I had made in my part.
I cannot now recall to mind every
instance in which I have remembered
the criticisms which have been written
upon me, — where I have instinctively
felt that they were right and I was
wrong, and I altered my part accord-
ingly. I have great admiration for
the writings of some theatrical critics,
who whenever they have to say anything unkind, do so in a very gentle-
manlike way and in a kindly spirit,
and who if they praise you, do so to
the utmost of their power. This, of
course, is in violent contrast with
those critics who are led, more or
less, by personal feeling of like or
dislike to the artist they are criticising, or with those people who make

it a point of turning everything into ridicule, no matter what you may attempt from a high-art point of view.

Certainly I think the love of the amateur world for theatricals, which has increased so much of late years, has done as much good for the stage as amateurs have done for music. Look at the amateurs who every night are seen at the Philharmonic concerts, who help to keep up the tone of high classical music by their devotion and their love of it. So I think amateurs have to a great extent helped the stage. No doubt, as with everything else, it has had its drawbacks. Amateurs come with their books, in the case of any play which they are going to do; and they sit in a private box and take notes, and give as near an imitation of anybody they think right, as they possibly can. At the same time there is the fact, that they are continually rehearsing, and that they each have their hero and heroine that they follow in the art. They are continually conversing in their own home circle as to theatres and theatrical life. It may have had its drawbacks, perhaps, in letting the outside world know that snow is made of pieces of paper, and that the moon is really only a limelight. At the same time it has, on the other hand, been the means of opening the minds of thousands in the world, who at one time had a sort of instinctive wonder at actors and actresses because they did not know them, and at the same time an instinctive dislike for what is termed going " behind the scenes." Nowadays all that is swept away. Everybody now knows how the curtain is taken up, and where the prompter stands, and what " flies " and " borders " are. Another very great thing for the public to have found out is that, as a rule, in from three to five minutes from one thousand to twelve hundred people may go safely out of a theatre. I am very proud to say that many of my friends have very often made their " first appearance on any stage " behind the footlights of the St. James's. All this converse and this reciprocal feeling between the audience and actors and actresses, and all this personal intercourse, has entirely swept away the thousand little cricks and prejudices which at one time existed ;

and I consider that it is the amateur who has, in great measure, opened the eyes of this section of the public.

On the opposite side of the balance must be placed the actors and actresses who instead of keeping to their art, take to society, and are more known for where they go in society than for their work upon the stage. There is an excellent anecdote told of Macready and Samuel Phelps. Macready was acting at Drury Lane in the West End, and Phelps at Sadler's Wells in the East End. Macready wrote a letter something like the following : —

MY DEAR PHELPS, — Why not come to the West, — a great actor like you? Surely there is room for two —

and so on. To which Phelps replied:

My dear Macready, — How kind of
you to think of me ! I am very happy at
the East End of London. I cannot act as
well *off* as I can *on* the stage, so I will stop
where I am.

This was written some number of
years ago. I venture to say that it
is a slight hit at some members of
my profession who make society a
vehicle for the stage, instead of making the stage a vehicle by which to
make society respect them. I shall
perhaps give offence by making these
remarks, and I apologize to those
whom it may hurt; but I feel this
deeply. When I know how hard
actors and actresses have to work,
and how often they have to change
their dresses at night; and when I
see them, tired and jaded, tearing
up to their dressing-room to put on

another dress, in order to go to some crush after the play, — I must say I feel it is a pity that any artists should think it necessary to air themselves before the eyes of that public which has paid its 10*s*. 6*d*. a few hours previously to see them. This, I know, is open to a great deal of contradiction, and many actors and actresses will say, " This is our relaxation. This is the time when our work is done, and we feel that we can go out and enjoy ourselves." And so it is. I have no doubt it has its good side, but from the point of view that I take, I doubt whether it will, in the end, do as much good as in the present day it is thought to do.

Because a person is charming at a dinner-table or at an evening party, people say, " We must go and see

So-and-so." It is a sort of thing that
creates curiosity, and people go to
the play because they have met the
artist in society. In fact, I look
upon it as a form of advertisement.
I may very likely be wrong. Some
people say I always *shall* be wrong.
Still, I have my poor opinion, and,
such as it is, I express it.

If artists really have exhausted
their energies upon the British public by acting parts which entirely
take every bit and drop of vitality
out of their fibre, they cannot shine
in society. They must either keep
to their theatrical work, or they must
reserve from the British public some
of their vitality, and retain it for the
good of society. If you are a bit-
terly conscientious person, and act
up to the hilt, I defy you night after

night to go out, after your work, or
even two or three times a week. If
an actor has a lengthy rehearsal during the day, and then has to play an
extremely heavy part, it is impossible
that he can go out again afterwards.
During the year that I played in
" Impulse," I went out to nearly every
party and reception to which I was
invited. But why? I had not forty
lines to speak in the whole play, —
nothing to do. I was fresh, and
equal to going out. But when I
have a heavy part, I could no more
go out than I could take wings.
Not that I am applying my observa-
tions to that point of view at all. I
am applying them to the fact that
there are many artists upon the stage
who go into society for the sake of
being seen, and by that means get

a sort of *clientèle* of the public who follow them on to the stage. That is what I dislike.

Great indeed is the compliment when the highest in the land seek the society of those who have done honor and credit to the stage; but there is no compliment when the seeking is prompted by curiosity, or merely responds to a desire for self-advertisement.

I do not think that amateurs take the bread out of other people's mouths. Since amateurs have come upon the stage, they have brought with them an immense deal of good. Look at the hundreds and hundreds of nice young girls — and young men too — who, with regard to personal qualifications, are certainly gifted for the theatre; it is perfectly wonderful the different people that I see who wish to come upon the stage, and I always encourage them to do so.

Women, as a rule, are quicker in learning anything than men. I do not think there is a thing in the world that a woman could be better than an actress; there is no other calling in which she can earn so much money, — no other calling in which she can keep her own standard so high; no other calling in which she can set a better example and do more good. An actress lives in a world of her own creation and imagination for the time being, — a world in which she is perfectly happy or perfectly miserable, as the case may be; and she holds a position which is unique if she has the necessary qualifications, — such as the perseverance which is necessary even when the talent is already there.

I do not say there is room for all, but those who have the ability will naturally come to the fore. Of course there must be a large majority who will go to the wall, poor girls! But at the same time there are a great many who come to the front, — at any rate there are a great many who can earn their £300 or £400 a year; and that is a very nice competence for a woman in the middle class of life, — very much more than she would earn in almost any other career. Besides, she has the blessedness of independence; and that is a great thing to a woman, and especially to a single woman.

Naturally many of the acting profession are in the ranks of the " unemployed." That must always be the case where there is a very large concourse of people; and in the dramatic profession the risks are increased by the hazardous and temporary nature of engagements.

There is a very great discussion as to whether people act best in parts that are most like themselves, or most like the people they would wish to be. This is a controversy that is continually being opened, and has never yet been answered. Some people think that if the part of a villain is acted very well, the actor must be a villain, and therefore anybody who plays the part of a murderer must be looked upon with aversion. To a small extent, there is no doubt about it, you must bring your own individuality and character upon the stage. That goes without saying.

I think success chiefly depends on the power of imagination and the creative faculty; and the question is whether it is developed enough, and whether you can throw yourself into the feelings of the character, whatever they may be at the time. A very severe critic once said that unless a woman was very, very noble in all the attributes of her life, she could not play a certain beautiful Shaksperian character. Well, that is a very severe stricture, because whatever a woman's life may be, that surely can have nothing to do with the bump of her imaginative faculty or creative power. But there is no doubt about it that we bring on to the stage an atmosphere of our own,

—that, I decidedly assert; whether in a large part or small one, the peculiar personal characteristics that we possess will show themselves.

In a paper read before the Social Science Congress some time ago, I said, " It is pleasanter to think that when the curtain has fallen, and the actor or actress is at home, he or she leads, or is capable of leading, the same kind of life." I meant by this, if any one had been playing some great and noble character that evening, and stirring all the better and grander emotions in our nature, we the public, who had been, for the time, carried out of our own lives, could reflect with satisfaction on the artist who had been gifted with so much power! In this instance I make myself one of the public. I

wear for the moment my crown as
" Matron of the Drama ! "

Old Absolute tells his son Jack to
get an atmosphere of his own. There
is no doubt that we all have our own
atmospheres and suns. We do not
drop them when we go into a drawing-room or into a dining-room;
therefore how can we possibly drop
them when we are on the stage?
This is all I mean, nothing more.
After all, it's only my opinion. (I
call these papers " Dramatic Opinions," that if I say anything likely to
wound, I may be forgiven. I set
down nought in malice, gentle reader;
 believe them not when they tell you
I do !) A man may put on a mus-
tache and whiskers, but there he is
underneath. A woman has even
greater drawbacks. She cannot put

on whiskers and mustaches, and be like the " bearded pard; " she must always have, within close limits, the same appearance. That is where a woman's work is so much more *diffi-cile* than a man's, because a man can outwardly entirely change himself. So complete is the transformation sometimes that I have seen an actor come on the stage whom I knew extremely well personally, and I have not recognized him at all, until he began to speak.

There are several amateurs whose make-ups are wonderful, but directly they open their mouths their voices naturally betray them. Very few es- tablished, recognized actors can play a whole part in a feigned voice. There are, of course, some who can do it, but as a rule the *voice* betrays.

And as we can but very seldom
sustain a feigned voice or give ourselves a different voice, so, in my
opinion, we cannot give ourselves a
different soul or a different body.
We must come upon the stage as we
are created. The power of our creative faculties and imagination may do
much for us, but we *are* what we are;
and again, I say, we bring our own
atmosphere with us.

Of course people will say that to
be a great artist you should be able
to put yourself and your feelings entirely on one side, and think only of
the part. For instance, some people
are very angry when one sheds real
tears. There have been a great many
arguments on this point. They say
you must make the audience feel,
and yet not cry yourself; and there

is no doubt one can overpower even one's own power by shedding too many tears, and by allowing one's feeling to overcome the more intellectual idea of the part. But it is a great blessing to a woman to have a good cry, and if some parts admit of it, where is the harm? Surely to see real tears in a situation where real tears would have sprung to the eyes must for the time give the audience the pleasure of feeling that the actress is at any rate in her part, even if at that particular moment, poor thing! she may have failed signally in arousing sympathy in the hearts of those who look at her.

The orchestra is a great part of theatrical life. Mr. Buckstone always asked the opinion of the orchestra

concerning a play which he was going to produce. As a rule, the orchestra is not called into a theatre
at rehearsals until the play is to some
extent smooth, and then, perhaps the
last week or two, the orchestra comes
in and plays the incidental music.
The men of the orchestra have not
been tired by seeing the play rehearsed, scene by scene and act by
act, and therefore they come fresh to
it. This circumstance, I suppose, in-
duced Mr. Buckstone always — during the last rehearsal — to advance
to the orchestra and say, " Now, gentlemen, what do you think of the
piece?" If it were a comedy and
the orchestra were heard to laugh,
Mr. Buckstone always said, " This is
all right, the orchestra see it and hear
it for the first time, and it is all right."

Or if the cornet-player raised himself from his seat to stand and look at a pathetic scene, Buckstone would turn round and say, " Ah ! that is all right ; the pit will like that." Mr. Buckstone had much belief in the judgment of the orchestra. I remember a certain leader of the orchestra once listening to a poetical play, and the author for a moment forgot his dignity and asked him, " What do you think of that ? " The leader of the orchestra was a timid little man, frightened to death of the author, and he turned round suddenly and said, " Oh, it is better than Shakspeare ! "

In some theatres — indeed in most of the large provincial theatres — the band plays the audience out until it disperses, as they do in church. Whether or not that is good, I do

not venture to say. I think the orchestra is a very great aid to any
dramatic action. People so love
music that unless it is dragged in
injudiciously, I think it must always
be an immense help to the audience.
I like to see an orchestra; but as I
so seldom sit among the audience, I
do not think I am in a position to
speak on this point. But it is a great
help to me to hear a little music, and
it seems to me a relief to my own
voice, of which, if I have a very long
part, I sometimes weary.

CHAPTER III.

VERY year we go on tour with our London company. One year we took " Impulse; " another year we played " Lady Clancarty."

We always go to Manchester, Liverpool, Glasgow, Edinburgh, Birmingham; sometimes to Dublin. Bristol I have been to twice since I was a little girl. Travelling on Sunday is very hard work, but, like everything else, it has its compensating charms. You can make a great deal of money by touring about in the country. The public know that you will be there only for a week or a fortnight, and they naturally all come to see you; and if you take a London success, you do brilliantly, according to your popularity.

The work is more than amusing, it is the greatest teacher in the world; because you have a different sort of audience in nearly every town. What is successful at Bristol may be a failure at Bath. What is cheered to the echo in Liverpool may perhaps not be so successful in Manchester. It

is very strange that audiences which
are so closely connected, have such
various opinions. Of course Manchester is our great stronghold, because we were married there, and I
think the people there have a sort
of affection for us; so I cannot help
speaking of Manchester first and fore-
most. Then, again, Glasgow is the
town where my husband began his
professional career, and there he is
received with acclamation. I suppose seldom has such an uproar been
heard as when he was discovered as
Charles Surface in the " School for
Scandal," on his return to Glasgow,
as the leading man of the Haymarket
company. The applause was so long
and so extraordinary that Mr. Buckstone had to come upon the stage
and stop it. My husband had begun

his career at £1 a week, and had left, having gained his position; and then he came back as the leading man of what was at the time considered the greatest company that ever travelled in the provinces.

A Scottish audience likes quite a different sort of play to what a Yorkshire or Lancashire audience would like. If you say in Scotland that you have a play "from the French," they appear a little shocked. Why this should be I do not know. It was in Edinburgh, I am sorry to say, that a gentleman wrote, saying he thought it was such a pity that such and such a piece from the French should be played. Why did not we play that beautiful English comedy of the "Queen's Shilling"? — which, I need hardly repeat, is from the

French, "Le Fils de Famille." If
in Scotland you put anything up by
Sheridan, or Sheridan Knowles, or
Shakspeare, or any well-known author within their circle of reading,
they know the piece just as well as
you do. They are a most marvellously well-read people. They are
most enthusiastic if you " get " them.
They are a long while taking to you,
but if you have them once, you have
them always. Look, for instance, at
that great actress, Lady Martin, —
Miss Helen Faucit, — who perhaps is
an example that all the profession
can follow, in every possible attribute
of womanhood. Long after she was
married she used, I believe, to visit
Glasgow and Edinburgh, where her
popularity was something unique,
and there she would play for a

month. They used to follow her more and more each time. Her art overpowered everything. They never thought of asking whether she looked King René's daughter, who is described in the first scene as "budding sixteen, with a bloom upon her cheek that childhood had only just parted from; with coral lips, and not a wrinkle on her brow." She came upon the stage to play King René's daughter long after she was sixteen; and the great Scottish multitudes rose at her, and their only regret was, as it must be the regret of all who have any knowledge of her, that she left the stage.

In Ireland things are quite different; there *c'est pour le jour.* That is exactly the difference between the Scotch and the Irish. I remember

playing in " Pygmalion and Galatea "
in Ireland, and when at the end of
the first act Galatea is going to throw
herself into the arms of Pygmalion,
telling him that she loves him, and
that she is his forever, a woman in
the pit rose up and said, " Whisht!
darlint! whisht! Don't kiss him, his
wife has just gone out."

The Irish are delightful. Their
enthusiasm is charming, but it is an
enthusiasm that is awakened by the
next comer the instant you have left.
Poetical as the Irish are, there is a
verse, written, I believe, by one of
their countrymen, the sentiment of
which does not seem to remain in the
elements of their nature, —

" If the refrain of some song I sang you,
    Or the perfume of some flower or tree
  Steals across your senses, may it bring you
  Silent messages of love from me."

7

Now, they do feel the refrain of the song, they do know the perfume of the flower and the tree, whilst you are there, and whilst you are singing the song; but it is " sweet, not lasting." If another singer comes the following evening and sings that song again, they are equally delighted.

But I must say that I never received anything but the greatest kindness and warm-heartedness from Irish people, and their hospitality is world-renowned.

The Manchester audience is an extraordinary one. There are Russians and Turks and Germans and French and Greeks. It is quite cosmopolitan. If one part of the house does not take one line or sentiment, another does. It is the most pulsating, rapid, inspiring audience to act to, and I do not think there is any artist in the world who would not pay a tribute to the spontaneity and quickness of a Manchester audience. Give me the Theatre Royal, Manchester, and a house crammed to suffocation, and I feel I do my best. Somehow, I think it is because I feel they like me very much, that I am able to do my best. If an audience expects you at your best, and gives you an impetus to bring out the best in you, you wish to keep up their estimation of you, and you strive to do your very utmost.

Some actors are so sensitive that when they come on the stage, if they are not received well, down go their spirits, and they never rise again the whole evening, — I know several instances of that; and, on the contrary, if they are well received, up go their heart and spirits, and they really give the audience their best.

Birmingham is another place I love; and when, on Saturday nights, all the miners and workpeople come from Wolverhampton and the surrounding districts, I think nothing is more exhilarating. They are so pleased with you and so delighted with everything you do, — and then you are pleased that they are pleased. The audience there is purely English.

Brighton is London in November; and a very delightful week we have there too. We get pretty much the same people as in London.

I have sometimes been asked to give the history of a play from the MS. to the stage. I may begin by saying that very few plays indeed have ever been acted before the public in the state in which they were originally brought into the theatre; they undergo a thousand changes. It often happens that a MS. is submitted which contains a very beautiful leading idea, but badly worked out. In such cases the manager becomes, as it were, a collaborator with the author. Many plays are altered in this manner. The manager makes suggestions, and the actors do the same when they come to rehearse, — receiving, of course, hints in their turn from the author; and so the work gets into shape.

Mr. Kendal and I get quantities of plays brought to us, and we make it a rule to read nearly every one of them. Of course, they are not all worthy of being placed before the public; but I am perfectly astonished

at the amount of good there is to be
found in the first plays of young
playwriters, — unknown young men
and women. There is perhaps one
scene that is remarkably good, or it
may be some leading idea or character, but so badly surrounded that the
play will not admit of production. I
always in such cases write back to
the author, "Go on; you have the
germ. Do not spare paper and ink
and trouble, and you will eventually
find that the good fairy has touched
you with her wand." I should think
in the course of a year we have hundreds of plays submitted to us. My
working table is covered with them,
and I have some cupboards full besides. A great many are comediettas

in one act, sent me by young ladies,
— sometimes translated from the

French or German, — pretty little
things often, but too light and flimsy
for use; containing, nevertheless, de-
cided germs of talent. I think the
matinées which have come into fashion are a very great boon. Of course
they are in some ways detrimental to
art, but they have many advantages
which more than counteract any harm
they may do. I have seen some
very bad plays produced at them, but
I have also seen some very good ones.
They afford an excellent means of
making the work of a young author
known.

I may as well confess that I am not
personally a good judge of a play or
of a part. I will tell you an instance
of my gross stupidity, by reason of
which I lost my husband and his
partner a very large sum of money.

I had sent to me, some long time ago, a play. I thought the idea was splendid, but I did n't like the way in which it was worked out. One scene I found, I may say, absurd; namely, that a man should sit down and forge his wife's name in her cheque-book, before her. I thought this was such a blemish in the play, and so ludicrous, and such a bad starting-point, that though the rest of the play was very clever, and the audience might forget that failing in it, still it would make a bad beginning, and would more or less ruin the rest of the play. I returned it to its author, and told him so. That play was produced at a *matinée*. It was an enormous success, and was eventually put into an evening bill, and made thousands. Let me here blushingly, and with the deepest contrition, say that that play was called " Jim, the Penman."

As a rule Mr. Kendal reads most of the plays sent to us. He is an excellent judge, and possesses the faculty of knowing exactly when there is money in a play. He is very difficult to please, and very seldom wrong; his judgment is so cool. As I have freely confessed my own fatal blunder, I may excuse myself by saying that I do not believe I am the only person who has erred in such matters of judgment.

I am sometimes asked whether we have ever made a success with a play that has been refused elsewhere. I could not be positive on the point, but I think it is more than probable that we have. Sometimes, what is finally submitted to the public is only

half what the author originally wrote.
A striking instance of this is Mr.
Smith's comedietta of " Uncle's Will."
We practically took only half the
piece; but I think we picked out all
the plums. Nearly the same thing
happened with regard to "Little Lord
Fauntleroy." When the play was
produced, Mrs. Burnett said to me,
"You have cut it about rather se-
verely." I ventured to remark that
had I cut any flowers out of the play,
I would humbly beg her pardon; but
that I thought I had only knitted my
cloth a bit finer, and by that means
brought out its brighter gloss. That
is, of course, only what habit gives
you the power of doing, — that, and
the instinctive feeling of what will be
more or less dramatic.

It is no easy task to " cut " well,

as we call it; that is, to be able to
make judicious omissions, — to leave
all the beauty, and only take out the
weeds; to separate the wheat from
the chaff; or, taking another meta-
phor, to gather the stitches together,
as we do with crewel-work.

Sometimes authors will leave plays
with us for three or four weeks, or for
as many months, and then, after a
little while, they write and ask us
whether we have read it, and what
our opinion is. We often write a
very detailed opinion, which sometimes is shown to other managers
and used as a lever. The number
of plays we manage to read in a
given time of course depends on
whether we are busy at rehearsal,
or have other things to do. As a
rule, my husband and I, every night

of our lives, read something or other, or I go through a book that perhaps will make into a play. When a manuscript has been accepted, it is in due course put into rehearsal. As a rule the authors are present at the rehearsals, and are very nervous, — which has rather a paralyzing effect on the actors. Authors differ a good deal in the way they regard the interpreters of their work. It often happens that one finds one's part too long, and then one "cuts" it oneself; or it is too short, and then one asks the author to "write in" a speech, or to elaborate a scene; and generally such requests are granted readily enough. Some authors, however, boast of writing plays which they are pleased to term "actor-tight," — meaning that the play is independent of the artists who interpret it; but I think that this way of looking at things is dying out, and that most authors will acknowledge that they owe something, at any rate a little something, to the actors.

My brother Tom always stage-managed his own plays, and I have always believed that he was a very clever stage-manager; every action and every idea of his being followed by the actors and actresses of the Prince of Wales's Theatre, who believed in him, — and of course, when people believe in you, you start fair.

I met Tom in his capacity as manager only once. That was when I played at the Gaiety in his comedy of "Dreams." I had a small part in that play, with Alfred Wigan and

Mr. Clayton; and it then struck me that my brother was a very gifted stage-manager; but I do not know whether my opinion in this particular instance is worth recording. One is apt, perhaps, to think well of one's relations; however, I think his excellence is acknowledged by all who knew him personally and who were connected with him professionally. I believe in his early life he had taken his plays from theatre to theatre; and it is believed that on the back of the MS. of his play called "Society," old Mr. Chippendale, of the Haymarket, had written the word "rot." Eventually Tom met Miss Marie Wilton, who, as all the world knows, gave him a first trial at the Prince of Wales's Theatre. He there made his name, and what money he left behind him. He was a particularly generous man. He had a certain sum per night for " Society," and a certain sum, which I believe was an increase on that, for " Caste; " and for " School " an increase again. When a number of years had rolled over, and the management wished to revive these plays, my brother was written to and asked (as he had now become an established author) what his terms would be for a revival of his plays; he wrote back and said, the same as he had always received. And when " Society " was revived some seven or ten years after he had made his reputation, he received the same small sum per night as he did before he was known. He was a most chivalric and generous-natured man.

Tom Robertson did not write all his plays for that management, but he felt himself more at home at the Prince of Wales's Theatre than anywhere else. Whenever he migrated to any other ground, he did not seem to flourish in the same way. I believe "Dreams" was a success at the Gaiety; but in those days I did not know much of the pecuniary positions of theatres, or their losses and gains. My chief impression of "Dreams" is associated with the fact that I had the pleasure and honor of acting with Mr. Alfred Wigan, who was a great artist and the kindest creature, so full of encouragement, and so wishful to tell you everything that was to your advantage. We used to sing a little duet in the course of the play; when he had a bad cold, and could not take

the high notes, I used to sing them
for him; and when I had a bad cold,
then he used to sing them for me.
It is altogether a very delightful remembrance in my life. The first
gold bracelet I ever received was
given to me by Mrs. Alfred Wigan.
Miss Ellen Farren, who played boy's
parts, was also a very great favorite
with Mr. Wigan. He used to take a
great interest in her career; but, poor
man! he died some short time after
that, and we lost a great artist and a
good friend. Nearly twenty years
had then elapsed since the period I
am speaking of, and then, before
Miss Ellen Farren went to Australia,
she wrote me a letter in which she
said she was bidding farewell to her
Gaiety audience, and would I not do
something for her?

I recited a few verses, written by Mrs. Oscar Beringer, just stating the fact that many years ago two young women (girls in their teens) had appeared upon the Gaiety stage, that one of them had gone away, but that one had remained true to Gaiety and the public, — *i. e.*, Miss Farren herself; and that, I thought, was a wonderful instance of how one could pass so many years of one's life upon a single stage. Miss Farren was at the wing whilst I recited these few lines about her. The audience were so carried away with enthusiasm that they persisted in seeing her again and again.

To return to my brother. When he began to make his name, I had not even come to London. The only "first night" I ever saw as a spectator at the Prince of Wales's was, I think, " School."

A very successful play of my brother's was " David Garrick," in which, I need hardly say, Mr. Sothern originally took the leading part. He made a very large sum of money by it, and I was very pleased the other day to hear that Mr. Wyndham had done the same. I hope it is true. Mr. Wyndham also bought another play lately, for a certain term of years, which my brother wrote for me when I was a girl, and which I once played in Hull for some five or six nights, — a very delicate, beautiful play, translated from Alfred de Musset's "On ne badine pas avec l'amour." I never have had the opportunity of playing it again, but Mr. Wyndham having bought nearly all my brother's plays to revive, made an arrangement with me to revive this too; and I am looking forward with great curiosity to hearing the result. It is, I think, one of the very best translations my brother ever did.

The public are always curious about money matters, and I am often asked whether playwriters make large fortunes. There is no doubt about it, they do. It is difficult to be precise without mentioning names, which of course would never do; so I will tell, speaking generally, how money is made.

Authors charge different sums of money for their works. If they are original works, they will sometimes sell them for so much down, and then so much a night; but I think authors holding high positions will take something like ten per cent, sometimes more, on the gross receipts.

A young fellow who gets his first piece acted, would probably get only £30 or £50 down; and there the manager who risks taking an unknown author gains the advantage. But directly a man has got his position, he charges, of course, what he considers he has a right to charge. There is no doubt you cannot open a theatre now unless you have a good play. Naturally these men, who know they draw the money, expect a part of the profits. I believe my brother had £1 a night for " Society; " but I know no man who now occupies anything like the position my brother occupied, who would allow his play to be played for that sum. It might be so with a comedietta, but with nothing else.

The salaries of actors have risen very greatly. I remember thinking that £10 a week, or £15 or £20 or £25, were enormous salaries, where now £60 and £80 would only adequately represent the same sort of talent, so extraordinarily have actors and actresses' salaries, as well as authors' fees, increased. Salaries were even different during the last year of the St. James's to what they were when the management of Messrs. Hare and Kendal began, only nine seasons ago. The same actor who would then get, we will say, £7 a week, would probably now ask £20.

As a consequence, the public pays 10s. 6d. for a stall, — which is a con-

siderable increase on former prices.
Then, too, by doing away with pits
and charging 10s. 6d. for all the seats
in the body of your theatre, you naturally can pay more to your artists.

In Birmingham and Manchester the
pit comes right up to the orchestra;
and I confess, though it may show
poor taste, that I delight in playing
to the pit. No one who is not in the
profession could tell what an exhilarating effect the pit has. I love it;
one gets such a quick response to
the sentiments we arouse. In the
stalls, people are impassive. It is the
height of good breeding not to show
one's feelings; and that is why actors
and actresses who do nothing but
show their own feelings, and other
people's too, are such peculiar, strange
people! Again I apologize for saying,

or daring to state, actors and actresses are peculiar or strange! Please remember it's only one of my opinions! There is no doubt about it, the pit is a delightful institution; there is much virtue in a pit.

Applause, however, in London theatres has more or less gone out, except on a first night, when a popular artist gets a "reception," as it is termed. In fact every artist gets a "reception" of some sort; and of course the verdict on the play is given by applause, which is more or less true in its ring, and in which I seldom have been mistaken. There may be a great deal of applause at the fall of the curtain on a first night, and many people round will say, "Oh, it's a success! It's a success!" but all the while there has

been something wanting in the ring
of that applause. While there is another applause that has got such a
hearty ring in it, so spontaneous, so
true, that it brings conviction with
it, and you feel the play is a success,
and that the applause is, as it were,
from the very hearts of the people.
That is what makes a first night in
London such a trial and such a nervous ordeal to go through, but at the
same time, if the result is good, such
a gratifying thing.

In the provinces they do give more
applause, I think. They applaud
their favorite, or any popular actor
who is in the company, whether it is
at a judicious moment or whether it
is not. It is the feeling that they
have for the artist, and they applaud
perhaps with more heartiness than

discernment. But oh, it is very nice! I like it to be lavish and indiscriminate. I like everything to be lavish and indiscriminate, especially applause!

Malicious people say that one sends one's friends in on the first night, and such things have been done; but I do not think the practice exists in any theatre that holds any position, nor do I believe that it has any weight in any way, because if they did applaud on the first night, the public would go on the second and third nights, and if the play is not good, it will not hold. Of course in Paris we know there is a *claque;* but I do not think a *claque* has ever been actually organized in this country.

In London there are what they call the " first-nighters " in the pit and

upper boxes; and woe betide the time
when the "first-nighters" do not
come, because I believe in their criticism more than any other, and in
their applause, and the reverse! I
could not tell you who the "first-
nighters" are, but I know that among
them I have got some friends, and
therefore I like them! They are
people who attend every first night
at every theatre. I myself have been
to only three first nights as a spectator in the whole of my professional
career, and when I go to the theatre,
then I invariably ask for the stalls in
the last row, that I may be near the
pit and hear their verdict,—so great
is my belief in the pit and its verdict;
I have seldom known it wrong.

The pleasure of acting depends, of
course, to a certain extent on the part

one happens to be playing; and one
feels some authors to be more sympathetic than others. This was the
case with my brother's plays, and I
should say the same of Mr. Pinero's.
I love to play in Mr. Pinero's pieces.
One has to speak the parts exactly
as they are written, down to the very
conjunctions! If you put in a different word, the line seems to halt. Mr.
Pinero writes, to my idea, charmingly.
His language is so wonderfully sympathetic that one cannot speak a
wrong word; the lines he gives
women, especially, in his plays are so
subtle and pretty. He seems to have
a sort of insight into the undercur-
rent of a woman's mind. In the psy-
chological study of a part like " The
Squire," and in that play which he
translated and adapted, " Le Maître

de Forges," he gives you an opportunity, if you can convey it, of suggesting an underlying sentiment in
all his words. This has often struck
me during the last act of " The
Squire." The poor heroine has to
part with the man she adores, — the
only man she has ever loved. In all
the crucial points of our lives the
most commonplace remarks rise to
our lips. Mr. Pinero has written a
scene in which he makes this woman
say, " Be a good fellow; go to bed
early ; go to church every Sunday,"—
a mere foolish commonplace; and all
the while the woman is laughing off
her grief, while the tears are running
down her face and she is suffering
agonies. Now, I have intense delight
in playing that scene, — it is so like
what I have passed through myself;

what I believe to be the inner and under current of a woman's life and feelings. One's outer life is so different to what one really thinks and feels! To me there is a sort of exquisite pain in playing that scene. I never can play it without crying.

That, by the by, is my great drawback, — I cry too much. I cry so much that I perhaps do not do my author justice; but that scene in "The Squire" is so wonderfully poignant and pleasantly painful to act. Sometimes the audience see this scene only from a commonplace, funny point of view; sometimes they laugh; and sometimes — and, thank God! more generally, for women feel the truth of a woman trying to be funny under such circumstances — they cry!

When an artist gets an author who
is *en rapport* with her feelings, who
she knows trusts her sufficiently to
allow her to play the part from her
own point of view, — more or less, of
course, under his guidance, — it is
perfectly wonderful how much more
she can do for that author and for
his play than she can for an author
who, giving nothing, expects a great
deal out of stories which seldom are
or can be human, and which when
they are human are so embittered
with Satanic satire that nothing that
is truly human can get in touch with
the subtleties of the author's mind.
I have met authors and authors, and
I speak as I feel.

I have taken parts as they came
in. I have never in my life been in
a position to have a play written

expressly for me, except the "White Lie," written by Mr. Grundy. I have never been anything else but an actress in a theatre who, when the author brought in a play, took what is called the "leading part."

Of course success is often, to a considerable extent, due to personal qualities, — personal appearance, we will say. But it must imply *some* talent. The public are not led only by beauty. Beauty will give an actress a favorable start, but I doubt if any woman, however beautiful, could draw an audience for long unless she had some other qualification. I should like to expatiate upon this point. I do not believe that beauty only would hold the public for over a month. There must be talent with it. There may be beauty, but there

must be talent. Lots of people say
that there are some beautiful women
whom the public go to see only for
their beauty. I do not believe that.
The public is too discriminating and
too quick; and although curiosity
might lead them to go and look at
a beautiful person, man or woman,
whose beauty only might draw them
there, it would not make them go
more than once, however beautiful
the person might be. In some instances extreme beauty has been detrimental to an actress. It positively
makes people think that it is her
beauty, and her beauty *only*, that is
drawing the public, when really she
ought to have the credit of its being
her brains and her intellect as well.
One may say of a certain actress, that
has been a drawback, because so

many people who want to say something disagreeable, declare, " Oh! it is only her beauty; " while in my humble opinion, were she not so beautiful, she would, by her talent alone, have held her audience. But her beauty is so overpoweringly exquisite that people give her credit for nothing else.

I should say that the sympathy of an audience is more readily awakened by a woman than by a man. But it would not be just to infer from this that the greatest dramatic artists have been women. Neither that nor the reverse would be true. If I had to make a distinction, I should say that  a woman brings more sympathy into a play, and a man more intelligence. If one were to make a list of the greatest actors and actresses, I think the honors would be pretty evenly divided between the sexes. A curious instance of the way in which keen interest may be aroused by the acting of men alone, occurs in the play " Diplomacy." The whole piece is wonderfully clever; but the most wonderful thing about it was that its great scene was played only by three men.

A discussion arose when that play was first produced as to whether it could possibly be a success, as the great scene in it was with men only. But it was an enormous success, and that scene was one of the cleverest ever written. Whether a theatre would be a success where all the actors were men, I do not say. I do not think it would be interesting, any more than I think it would be in-

teresting if a theatre's company were
composed only of women. I have
often thought that in contradistinc-
tion to the scene of the three men, I
should like to see a scene with three
women only, where they might discuss men. I would not leave the
men out of the question entirely. I
have often wondered whether a
scene between three women could
be made as powerful as the scene
in "Diplomacy."

Of course, every dramatic artist
forms a somewhat different ideal of
art. Mine is that everything should
be, as it were, spiritualized. For instance, when in "Henry VIII." Queen
Katharine is dying, she is supposed
to see a vision of angels. I believe
the scene used to be so arranged that
a lovely wreath of flowers or halo of

glory was passed from hand to hand,
until it came to the angel nearest to
Katharine, and the angel held it over
the dying queen's head. Katharine
wakes up with this lovely vision in
her mind. My notion of such a
death is that it should be serenely
happy; the queen lying with a smile
upon her lips, hearing the voices of
angels calling her, showing us the
last moments of a noble woman — a
suffering, grand nature — lifted in the
extreme moment of death's agony
into such blissful visions of the future
that she dies with a smile on her lips.
There are artists who would wake up
from that vision, tear their dress open,
gasp, gurgle in their throat, and try
to die with a death-rattle in it, showing the public the realistic and horri-
ble agonies of death.

But this would not be my idea of good art. The only suitable occasions for representing the horrors of death on the stage would be when the man had been playing the villain, or the woman had been bad, so that there would be a moral in the fact that he or she suffers agonies even in quitting this life; but where the artist has to realize before the public a good and noble character, and has seen a vision of heaven, then I would try to bring before the minds of the audience a marvellously peaceful and beautiful death, as the one last glorious moment of a beautiful life, — such would be my teaching through dramatic art. There are so many things taught on the stage. Let us sometimes teach the highest, or at any rate let our art be the striving after

the highest. Even if we do not suc-
ceed, let us be humble votaries at
that shrine.

I find that people are often sur-
prised at the way in which actors
remember their parts; but this is not
so wonderful as it seems. The memory can be cultivated, like any other
faculty, up to a certain pitch. Practice works wonders. If you have not
played a part for years, the re-read-
ing of it, three or four times only, will
bring it back to you. We have so
much to help our memory on the
stage; we have what is called the
" business " of the scene. The fact
that you have to do certain things
brings a certain line back to your
memory. Often when you enter
your house, and sit at the same place
and at the same table, the memory of

the past returns. " C'est la même
chose sur la scène." A little bit of
business brings back a speech; the
remembrance of a speech brings back
a bit of business: the one helps the
other. Still, though an exceptional
memory is not absolutely necessary,
it is an enormous help.

The most extraordinary instance
of memory that I personally remember was that of old Mr. Buckstone, who used to come upon the
stage at rehearsal, reading his part,
and not knowing a word; but he
would come on at night, and the
clothes and the situation and the
whole thing brought the words back
to him. I am speaking of the repe-
tition of an old part. The fact of
putting on the clothes, and dressing
for the part, and speaking about it

a little, brought it back. He was most delightful to act with, so sympathetic in the way that he never took advantage of anybody on the stage being wrong; he was always so helpful, always so willing. He was a little deaf, and he learned his cues by the lips. That was one reason why he was very fond of the old faces around him, because he knew when they finished speaking, even if he could not hear them.

CHAPTER IV.

THERE is a great deal of difference, in my opinion,
between enthusiasm and
enthusiasts. There are enthusiasts,
and there is enthusiasm; the lat-
ter holding much longer to firm
ground than enthusiasts. An enthu-
siast is an actor or actress such as

one occasionally meets who is delighted with a new part, with new
clothes, with a new creation, and
while the excitement is on, loves it;
but when the first five or six weeks
have passed, gets tired of both part
and play, and longs for " pastures
new." The persons who, in my idea,
realize enthusiasm, are the individuals
who, acting night after night, never
allow their interest in their parts to
cease, who are neither influenced by
fair, bad, or good houses, but who are
always trying to amplify their parts
and who go on still trying to do
something more. Of course this may
be carried to a fault, as much as anything else, because you may over-
elaborate, and that is very bad
(over-elaborating, I may mention, is
a personal failing of my own), since,

in over-elaborating a play, you often lose the spontaneity which of course is the great charm. We all of us, more or less, run into one of these extremes, — either over-elaborating a part, or becoming indifferent to it; that is my idea of the difference between enthusiasts and enthusiasm. If I were one of the public and wanted to see a play at its very perfection, I should go to see it when it had been played three weeks (I speak, of course, of a successful play), when the excitement had not died out, and when it had not been played sufficiently often for people to become indifferent, but the enthusiasm proper still continued.

If an audience is very attentive to a play, they get the very best that an artist can give them; while, on

the contrary, if you feel the public
are not with you, you become self-
conscious, and can do nothing. One's
feeling of the audience is more a
general impression than noticing particular persons. Sometimes one no-
tices more, sometimes less. The only
people that I can see in a theatre are
those who are very near to me, — the
people in the first row or two of the
stalls, and the people in the private
boxes. I always feel very conscious
· of them, because they seem to be so
near; but otherwise one can have no
judgment of the effect one is pro-
ducing, because one cannot see — at
least, there are only a very few people with long sight who can see —
all over the house. But you can
instinctively *feel* whether the people
are listening to you, or whether you

are gaining their attention. I never had but one instance in my life of a man who was so bored by my interpretation that he yawned loudly through it; and it was at the first production of "The Squire." A man came into the stalls rather late, and looked about a good deal, and yawned so markedly, one could not avoid noticing him. It was very trying, but at the end of the second act he went out altogether, and did n't return. That little episode made me cry for about three days. It made me unhappy, and it recoiled upon myself, because I felt that had I been right, I must have gained his attention more than I did.

To revert for a moment to the incomes of actors. They are almost always over-estimated. The other

day a man sent my husband a play
from Germany. He said, " I know
you have £6000 a year private property; under these circumstances I
want so much for my play."

I have often been asked what is
my favorite performance. That is
a question I am unable to answer.
You fancy yourself in some particular
thing, but it is not always that in
which you most fancy yourself that
you do best, or which has the best
effect upon your audience. We may
sometimes attempt to work out a
very charming subtlety or idea, and it
does not reach the audience; or, *vice
versa*, we sometimes may, by the
simplest thing, produce an effect
which we are unconscious of. That
is just the chance of sympathy between yourself and the audience. It

is not possible, either, to judge by results, and lay down a rule that if a play has proved successful, it must have been a good performance. I always think you act best what you would like yourself to be. As Adelaide Proctor says, " We always can be what we might have been." That is my idea of the standpoint of art. If I am impersonating the character of a high-minded woman, it is what I should like to be; and I always fancy my wish is so strong that it makes me impersonate that part best. This makes it impossible for one to judge oneself of what one's best performance is. When you feel most at your ease, and least self-conscious, you are told for the following ten days after the production of the play that this is perhaps the most disappointing of all your performances.

It is a matter of opinion as to whether the Press controls the public. I am sometimes asked whether I consider that when the public hear that adverse criticism of a great favorite actor, the public keeps away. That is only answered by the question, Does the British public slavishly follow the opinions of the Press? In some cases, Yes; in some cases, No. Should the artist be strong enough to withstand all this, and if his or her popularity with the public goes far beyond the criticism; or if, again, the artist takes to heart what the Press has said, and tries to improve, — all this may, or may not, be obviated. One of the greatest favorites of the public and the Press has lately not

succeeded in a *rôle*. The Press has
been very adverse, and departed
from its usual tone when criticising
a performance of this artist; but
whether that has any influence with
the public, I, who am not in the
theatre, cannot say. I cannot say
whether the artist to whom I refer
has suffered pecuniarily. Some of my
friends say, " Take no notice ; the
world goes on rapidly. What has
been read yesterday morning, is forgotten to-morrow. The public go
to the theatre. They forget what
was the criticism that has been passed
upon the play, therefore do not worry
yourself. It hurts, it wounds ; but
it goes no farther than your own
vanity." Other people say to me, " I
did not go to such and such a performance, for it was abused in the

papers." Therefore I say, it is an open question whether a given artist is sufficiently strong in his or her position with the public, and whether the Press has or has not paramount influence. Nowadays, when everybody goes to the play, and when the public themselves judge more than they used to do, the theatre is becoming more a universal entertainment. In some instances artists have been found fault with, and the public have been enchanted, and *vice versa;* you can never arrive at the bottom of the question. I have known a play continue to run a hundred nights in spite of adverse criticism. If a play goes with the audience, and the Press praises it as well, the combination is extremely good, because the pulse of the Press goes with the heart of the public, and then " strength is victory."

Of our own plays, I think " Impulse " was the greatest success pecuniarily that we ever had. I say this in •an unbiassed spirit, as I played an extremely small part in it. The success was mainly due to Miss Linda Dietz, who played the sentimental part, and to my husband, who had *the* part of the play.

Now, here is an instance of a strange peculiarity of the Press. All the modesty of my family has departed from me. I am not modest, and I believe it must have gone out of my soul and entered into my husband's when I became his wife; for a more modest artist than he, could not possibly breathe. He played that part for an entire year;

he brought to the coffers of the St.
James's Theatre, through his marvellous performance, a considerable sum
of money, — perhaps as much as any
actor has been known in his life to
bring in the same space of time. But
no one ever wrote sheaves of praise of
my husband. If he had been one
of those men who could ever speak
of himself, this, perhaps, would have
been impressed upon the mind of the
public; but as he cannot do that, he
lives in the admiration of his wife
and children. The silence of the
Press made no difference to the
coffers of the St. James's Theatre, I
am proud to say; and therefore our
mutual admiration party was one of
jollity and sincerity, and had its
wings tipped with gold. I wish I
could tell you, or remember, some of

the love-letters Mr. Kendal received during the time he enacted this brilliant artilleryman. The anonymous letters would fill books, and they used to afford the most intense amusement to all of us.

I should say that Mr. Pinero and Mr. Sidney Grundy are the most popular English playwrights of the present day. Mr. H. A. Jones is a man of high position. Mr. Robert Buchanan is a very, very clever man. Of course the most poetical writer that we have is Mr. Wills. I have acted in only one play by Mr. Wills, "William and Susan." Few are sufficiently gifted to realize all that this writer's exquisitely poetical language admits of! It is a positive recreation to speak his lines. How simple, how pathetic, was that tiny part of the old woman who comes to hear tidings of her sailor boy! The poor lad is dead, and William has to break the sad news to her. I shall never forget the first time I heard that scene. The prayer, too, spoken by Susan, is a masterpiece of writing. It is always a subject of regret to me that this one play has afforded the only opportunity I have had of trying to interpret Mr. Wills's language and ideas, for which I have the greatest admiration, I may almost say reverence.

Mr. " Bolton Row " and Mr. " Saville Row " excited a great deal of curiosity when " Diplomacy " was first announced. Since then I have acted in a one-act play called " The Cape Mail," by Mr. Clement Scott, which gives a great opportunity to an emotional actress; but it is always difficult to put a delicate little play of half an hour's duration in an evening's programme.

Mr. Stephenson's "Impulse" is too well known to need comment from me, and that touching song, "Let me dream again," and the comic opera "Dorothy," will endear him to all musical amateurs.

We opened the St. James's Theatre with the "Queen's Shilling," which my husband had produced some seasons previously at Manchester. Mr. Godfrey's play of "Queen Mab" was written long before. His heroines are always pleasant to act, full of life and spontaneity. I was the original Lilian Vavasour in "New Men and Old Acres," the joint author of which, Mr. Dubourg, wrote a comedietta,

" Twenty Minutes under an Umbrella," which was a great success; and he paid me the compliment of dedicating to me his five-act romantic play of " Vittoria Contarini."

What can I say of Mr. Theyre Smith, whom all the world acknowledges? Amateurs will surely place wreaths of laurel round his brow, for " A Happy Pair " and " Uncle's Will " have been the cause of many pleasant parties, many flirtations, and more marriages than any other two pieces I can think of.

And now for Mr. Sidney Grundy. Of course I like his plays; who does n't? We produced his first comedietta at the Haymarket, " A Little Change," and his last play, " A White Lie." He is one of those authors who must positively have his

exact words spoken; his lines are
so terse and epigrammatic, they do
not admit of one word being inter-
polated by the actor. He always
writes me the *rô.'e* of a very high-
minded, noble-hearted woman (I
think I have already said, one often
acts the antithesis of one's own character best). Mr. Grundy is, I must
tell you, a very gallant man, and has
known me for a long time; and
thirdly, he comes from Manchester.
I can offer no other explanation of
why he always assigns to me such
womanly, beautiful characters, — unless, indeed, he means to convey a
sly hint to me to endeavor to become
like them in real life. As Lord Tennyson makes Ulysses say, " I am a
part of all that I have met." I have
met a great many authors, and they

have invariably been generosity and
kindness itself, generous in all their
dealings with me and with my husband (for man and wife are one;
when I write *I*, I mean *we*, and
when I write *we*, I mean *he*), — all
except one!

If I am asked how children on the
stage are treated by grown-up actors,
I reply that I have never in my life
seen anything but uniform kindness;
they are encouraged in every possible
way. Bulwer Lytton, in one of his
books, says that if you wish to be *en
rapport* with all the world as it is of
to-day, you should live with old
people when you are a child, and
live with children when you are old.
Therefore I believe that you must
take children and surround them
with the atmosphere and the treat-

ment of art from childhood if you wish them to be artists. Whether that will ever develop art in them, depends upon the individual character. In many instances it does so, especially with women; and as boys are fathers of the men, I do not see why the same should not hold good with *girls!*

I do not think it is an absolute law that great actors *must* begin as children, but as a rule, the enormous influence exercised upon the mind by what becomes habitual in the most receptive period of life cannot be replaced by later training. It has been said that no one can hope to make a first-rate violin-player who has not begun to study the instrument as a little child; and so it is, in my opinion, with acting. If you take a very

mobile girl of seventeen and make
her work hard until she is twenty,
you may mould her into an actress;
but if she does not begin until then,
she will find it very uphill work.   On
the other hand, how easy it will be
for " Little Lord Fauntleroy " —
Vera Beringer — to play a boy.   Directly I found she was to play a boy,
she was put into trousers, that her
movements might be those of a boy,
that she might put her hands in her
pockets and walk in boyish fashion.
I rehearsed her in trousers, so that
when the child came before the public she did not feel that she was
dressed in anything unusual.   If you
want to wear classic dress and to have
the peculiar movements that are necessary to carry the classic robes, you
must wear them when you are suffi-

ciently young not to know that you have got them on. If I thought one of my children was capable of going on the stage, — for I should like them to do so, if they have talent for it, — I should certainly make them begin early.

Little children do not feel shy and awkward. How can they? In " The Squire," the part of a village child was given to a girl about four years old. I said to the little creature, " Now, when I ask your name, I want you to say ' Stores' very loudly; and if you say it very loudly and very nicely, every night you will get an orange." She simply shouted it; I never had to tell her twice. She probably did not know in the least what " Stores " meant. But she got her orange, and ended by making the theatre reverberate with her voice.

Audiences always delight in witnessing the performance of children. There is something peculiarly attractive in the charm that youth, extreme youth, brings to everything. What can be more beautiful than a graceful little girl acting some pretty childlike part?

What a duck of a thing that little girl was in " Partners "! I loved to see her. It was all I could do to keep from jumping out of the box and kissing her.

Since then, this little child I so admired — " Minnie Terry " — has acted with us in " A White Lie." She only rehearsed a week, she was so quick, caught up every idea, every

intonation of the voice; she is even
better in health, so her mother told
me, when she is at work. She rests
all the afternoon, and looks forward
with joy to the evening's amusement;
for to children the theatre is a delightful place, — full of friends who
pet them before and behind the curtain. Another delightful performer
was little Miss Clitherow, in " The
Silver King."

Then, too, the talent of the grown-
up actor can, as I have said, generally
be discerned in the child. Although
the little monkeys only try to imitate
their elders, they have their own way
of doing it, — some better, and some
worse.

Often, of course, we are disap-
pointed afterwards. Lots of children
have been brilliant while young; but

then if they exhaust their stock of brains, it is like the wearing out of a clock's works, which once exhausted, can never be repaired.

Again, there are children and children. There are thousands of plays in which none appear; and when you want a child, it is sometimes most difficult to find a clever one. There was a child, of about four, the boy in " William and Susan." We used to teach him to play with his little boat and to say, " Ay, ay, your honor." Sometimes we had the most dreadful trouble. One morning he would not do it at all, while the next he would be ready with his " Ay, ay, your honor," at the right moment. If you employ a child so young, you must take the consequences. I had to look at him if he forgot, and give him a little touch; then perhaps he would say " Ay, ay," so confidentially that the audience would not hear. Another time he would burst it out at the top of his voice.

Of course even the smallest children must soon get beyond this. Then before long comes the time when they are neither little children nor grown up, and when there is nothing for them to do.

Six or seven is a common age for a child to go on the stage. When they have been in the theatre for a year or two, and are eight or nine, they begin to take great interest, and an intelligent interest too, in the profession. They are very old-fashioned, from always being with their elders. They naturally must dress in the room where " grown-ups " are, and

their minds become prematurely advanced. Thus throughout their lives
they give the impression of being
older than their years. I have experienced this myself. I have been
on the stage since I was a child.
Suppose a case of a woman of my
age who was not an actress, and who
began her career at twenty, instead
of, as I did, at three. How much
younger her mind would be than
mine! How much more room there
would be in it! With me the feelings, sensations, experiences which
pass through my heart and try to
find relief in words are so merged
one into another, so crowded and
tumultuous, that fast as I talk,
I cannot express the half of
them.

But to return to the children: their

grand time is in the pantomime season, when enormous numbers are
employed.

And what an excellent thing! Oh,
think of the families at Christmas
that are positively kept from starv-
ing by the fairies' weekly stipend!
Think of fairies, and then think of
dinner, — so unfairylike! But oh,
what joy! Could any fairy of Hans
Andersen's creation give more joy
than the flesh-and-blood fairy of the
stage, when on Saturday mornings
she takes 15*s.* or 18*s.* to the mother,
and there is meat for dinner on Sun-
days! What else in the world but
a fairy at Christmas time can do
that? Then fancy the bacon which
they have lived on all the rest of the
year disappearing, and mutton taking
its place! Look how beautifully the

poetry of life can be elicited even from the pantomime! The duke's child sits in front in the dress-circle and feasts its eyes upon the fairies in all their glory; but what are its feelings compared to those of the poor mother who sees the fairy come home, wingless and uncrowned indeed, but bringing in her hand the well-earned salary? That is the joy the pantomime gives to me, who sometimes go behind the scenes. Then think of the kindness, the uniform kindness, of actors and actresses to these children: there is nothing under the sun too good for them. There are such noble things done that outsiders would be amazed at the record. Far be it from me to advocate that children's whole lives should be passed in a theatre, but there are times when it can do nothing but good; and when you come to think that managers who produce pantomimes sometimes engage as many as 150 little children, to none of whom they ever give less than 12s. a week, it will not surprise you to hear that hundreds of children are seen waiting at the stage-door of Drury Lane and Covent Garden and the Standard at Christmas time.

It is sometimes urged that harm comes to the children. But what does this amount to? Of course they have late hours, but when they do get home, they have plenty of time for sleep. Then, of course, the School Board interferes nowadays. People frequently come to me and ask my opinion upon certain matters connected with the employment of

these children. They want to know
what I think of their being taken
away from school and made to play
in the pantomimes and to rehearse,
considering that it constitutes a serious interference with their education.
I reply, My dear ladies, I really do
not know anything about that. But
this I do know, that by giving children the recreation of going to a
theatre and dancing, you are pro-
viding for them an immense pleasure; you employ them in a childish
pursuit, and you enable large numbers to make merry together. Why,
the dancing-mistress at Drury Lane
is simply worshipped by the children.
Again, the manager, as a rule, if he
keeps them certain hours over time,
will give them food. And when they
return home, the little child of the

lowest and poorest woman in the
world will certainly be looked upon
and treated with more urbanity and
kindness for being the bread-winner.
Even where the mother is neglectful,
the knowledge that this is the child
who brings money home, rather than
the child whom she has to supply
with a penny for school, will make
a difference. And if they have to
go through the rain and sleet and
snow to the pantomime, must they
not do the same to go to school?—
with this difference, that at the end
of the second week of the pantomime,
the mother will have money enough
to buy her child a waterproof. At
the pantomime, the wages are often
12s. a week; and this is as much as
a laborer gets in many parts of the
country. It is true that when the

pantomimes are over, the children have to return to their *moutons*, or rather want of *moutons;* but they have all had several weeks of profitable work, and that is so much to the good, and may balance the few cases where, as the good ladies would say, the little heads have got filled with "inflated theatrical notions," — perhaps even the serious disaster of having lost their places in the class!

It may be it has its evil sides. No doubt it has. They acquire a silly love of admiration, and there is the reaction after parting with the kind friends they have made. But often the friends they have made in the theatre are able to help them in after life.

I may be told that however correct my views are with regard to the children who perform at the pantomime, the conditions under which young people of a better class begin their career are very different. I am told that if my own children went upon the stage, they would be looked after far more closely, and that I should admit the existence of a number of bad influences which I should take uncommonly good care to keep them out of. I entirely deny this. What influences would there have been, for instance, at the St. James's Theatre that I should have had to keep my girl out of? Whom would she see? There are the same influences behind the scenes of a theatre as there are in a drawing-room. If a girl is pretty, weak, and vain, and some man says to her, "I love you," those magical words will, as long as the world goes round, turn the heads of *some* girls, and have no effect upon others. I do not care whether they are sitting behind the scenes in a theatre, in a drawing-room, in a ball-room, in a lodging-house parlor, or anywhere else, the words will take effect or not, according to the ground they are thrown upon. They may be said to an unresponsive ear and an unresponsive heart, or they may be said to an ear, a heart, a soul, that are responsive. It would depend entirely upon the impression on the girl's heart at the moment whether any echo of the words reverberated in her soul. It does not signify *where* or when these words are spoken. It is the magic sympathy of one life with another that decides their influence.

Consider, too, what love-making on the stage really means. A young girl comes into a theatre to play *ingénue* parts. She stands in the wing ready to be called upon the stage, and she sees a man and a woman making love. The man says, " Dearest, fly with me." The woman says, " I dare not." The man says, " We will go at once. Come." The first time such words as those fall on the ears of a young girl unaccustomed to them, they might, if said with fervor and passion, mean something; but as a rule something of this sort occurs. As soon as the words, " Dearest, fly with me," are uttered, they are interrupted by, " No, no, no ! " from the stage-manager; " when you say that, you stand at the back of the chair, you lean over Miss

Snooks's back; she waves her hand against you. Now, try it."

This is gone over twenty times, until at last the idea of " Fly with me," as understood by the young *ingénue*, must be of a most appalling kind. The gentleman has had his right arm, his left arm, his right leg, his left leg, his back, his chest, both his hands, his head — all talked over. He has tried it in a high voice, he has tried it in a low voice, he has tried it in a thin voice, he has tried it in a heavy voice, until there is no sense left of what " Fly with me " might under other circumstances mean. All the romance of love-making is gone. Therefore, what effect can it have? In love, is it not the fact that some of the charm lies in treating of an unknown land?

Since writing the above, the bill about which so much discussion took place has passed, and children are forbidden to act, or do any kind of work in a theatre, until they are ten years of age! But this will of course be reconsidered, and *well* considered.

What says the poet? "What would the world be to us if the children were no more!" Fancy pantomimes without children, without fairies! Fancy any one's life without fairies! Don't we all know it's the fairies who whisper the good things to us? Every human creature carries a tiny fairy in his or her heart, who whispers messages of hope, ambition, and love. Now fancy "lovers" without a fairy to fetch and carry pretty speeches one to the other! All the pretty tales we have

told our children about the "good
deeds" of the good fairies will be
dispelled, unless at Christmas-time
they can *see* the fairies creep out of
the flowers and rise out of the water
in the moonlight, and dance, and
prove all that their mothers have told
them is true! What will poor
mothers do when their babies are ill,
and "Oh, tell me a fairy tale!" is
swept away? What will the district-
visitor fall back upon if Cinderella
cannot have a fairy godmother? And
all the tales become *facts* when Christmas is here, and the fairies are actually
to be seen, — *seen* at the theatre!

Then please, dear, good, kind gentlemen, don't deprive us of them.
Why, how could Titania and
Oberon have ruled their court without their changeling? Certainly they

did quarrel about him, and have a difference of opinion like wretched mortals; but still, he *united* them again! Titania summons all her little fairies to scratch Bottom's ears and delight his eyes. Then how can we believe in Caliban if we cannot believe in the fairies? And oh, above all, don't deprive us of Prince Arthur! If you deprive us of Prince Arthur, you deprive us of a lesson of love and faith that men, women, and children can all understand, sympathize with, and delight in. Then the two princes! Only the seeing of Richard the Third makes us more and more appreciate Sir John Millais's picture of the two frightened little fellows clinging to each other, because please remember that though the Prince of Wales was a *big* boy, yet the Duke of York was only a baby less than ten, and if you see an older child, half your sympathy is gone.

Then again, Puck. Oh, really, you must *not* deprive us of Puck! Why, lovers would no longer quarrel and make it up without Puck to show us how he led them " up and down," and threw dust in their eyes.

Imagine that jolly old knight, Sir John Falstaff, without Little Robin as a contrast; or Banquo's going on his journey without Fleance! Why, you destroy Macbeth's chief ambition, and upset all his future arrangements. *This can never be!* Not many plays of Shakspeare could be acted.

And oh, horror of horrors! what would become of *me*, the " *domestic* actress," who can do nothing without a baby? At least, so Mr. Punch says, and *he* ought to know, for he has a great many of his own, so is a good judge!

But seriously, this question of not allowing children under ten years of age in a theatre is not to be lightly thought of. These " Baby fingers, waxen touches, weigh upon the actors' rest" (humble apologies to Lord Tennyson will follow); for the drama cannot live without its children, and the kind people who, with the best intentions, have taken up this question will assuredly be taught they are wrong.

There are, of course, many points for and against; but I am all for "for." With few exceptions, nearly all the actors and actresses who have

" achieved greatness " have begun early in life. *Before* they were ten years old, the first germ of their talent has been seen. If I dare mention names, I could give example upon example; but now I am packing up for America, and thinking of the ocean, and — now, if I were that funny man Mr. Punch, should n't I write something here about a " Water Baby? " — and saying *Au revoir* to my friends. Like these papers, I must leave to you, my dear, kind, gentle readers, the settling of this great question about our dramatic offspring! Deal gently, justly with them, and oh! deal *more* than gently, *more* than justly with these silly scraps of " Dramatic Opinions," jotted down just as they came into my silly head; for —

"Strong gales keep the clouds from raining ;
   Work lulls the sad heart's complaining."

And my heart is sad often, and sadder still at saying good-by to you who have helped me with your encouragement and applause (for I address my reader as a playgoer). With one more apology to a poet, —

"Be to my good points *more* than kind,
   And to my faults — why, blind, blind,
      blind !"

www.ingramcontent.com/pod-product-compliance
Lightning Source LLC
Chambersburg PA
CBHW031156050726
47495CB00019B/2173